THE TWIDDLE TWINS' MUSIC BOX MYSTERY

by HOWARD GOLDSMITH

illustrations by CHARLES JORDAN

For Ana Garcia Vasquez and Annie Rodriguez—H.G.
For Zoe—C.J.

For information contact:
MONDO Publishing
One Plaza Road
Greenvale, New York 11548
Visit our web site at http://www.mondopub.com

Designed by Christy Hale
Production by The Kids at Our House

Printed in the United States of America
97 98 99 00 01 02 03 9 8 7 6 5 4 3 2 1

Library of Congress Cataloging-in-Publication Data
Goldsmith, Howard.
The Twiddle twins' music box mystery / by Howard Goldsmith ; illustrations by Charles Jordan.
p. cm.
Summary: While trying to determine who stole their music box, the Twiddle twins find unusual clues such as banana peels, a coconut shell, and a chocolate bar wrapper.
ISBN 1-57255-475-4 (pbk. : alk. paper)
[1. Burglary—Fiction. 2. Monkeys—Fiction. 3. Mystery and detective stories.]
I. Jordan, Charles, ill. II. Title.
PZ7.G575Twe 1997
[E]—dc21 96-38005
CIP
AC

Contents

The Night Burglar

CREEEAK! CREEEAK!

The noise came from downstairs.

A *burglar*! thought Timothy Twiddle. His ears stood straight out from the sides of his head.

CRASH!

A *noisy burglar*, thought Timothy.

Timothy's door burst open. He shot out of bed and hit the ceiling.

"It's only me," said Tabitha, Timothy's twin sister. "You can come down now."

Timothy plopped down onto his bed. "Shhh!" he whispered. "There's a burglar downstairs."

"I know," said Tabitha. "Do you think I'm deaf?"

TINKLE. TINKLE. TINKLE.

The house filled with music.

"A musical burglar," said Tabitha.

"That's our music box!" Timothy cried. "Quick, let's go!"

Tabitha and Timothy raced into the hallway. Timothy crashed into their father. Tabitha bumped into their mother. All four landed on their backs, their feet in the air.

"Stay calm!" Mr. Twiddle pleaded. "There's a burglar downstairs!"

TINKLE. TINKLE. TINKLE.

Mr. Twiddle ran down the stairs with the others close behind. He threw open the door to the family room.

A dark figure leaped out of the window and disappeared into the night.

The Music Box is Missing

"Who was it?" Mrs. Twiddle cried.

"I couldn't tell," said Mr. Twiddle. "It was too dark to see."

"It must have been a cat burglar," said Timothy.

"Did he burgle our cat?" asked Tabitha.

"Where's Clarabel?" asked Mrs. Twiddle, pulling Mr. Twiddle's sleeve.

MEEEOWWW!

Clarabel peeked out from under the desk.

"Clarabel is hiding. She must have heard about cat burglars," said Tabitha.

"Look what Clarabel is wearing," Timothy cried. "Where did she get that cap?"

"The burglar must have dropped it," said Tabitha, turning the cap over in her hands.

"What do you suppose the letters JJ stand for?" Timothy asked.

"They must be the burglar's initials," Tabitha said.

Mrs. Twiddle looked around the room. "This place is a mess," she said.

A lamp and chair were knocked over. Books were lying all over the floor. A painting of Mrs. Twiddle's Aunt Matilda was about to fall off the wall.

"Here's my stamp collection," said Mr. Twiddle, picking it up off the floor.

"Look," Tabitha called out. "Here's half a banana."

"And a piece of coconut," said Timothy.

"And half a chocolate bar," Tabitha added.

"Where's our music box?" Mr. Twiddle yelled.

"The burglar took it!" everyone cried.

"Why would anyone steal our little music box?" Mr. Twiddle wondered out loud. "It's not valuable. My stamp collection is worth much more."

"The burglar must be a music lover," said Tabitha.

"A music lover who also loves bananas, coconuts, and chocolate bars," said Timothy thoughtfully.

"What a strange burglar," said Mrs. Twiddle.

Mr. Twiddle phoned the police. Soon Officer Wiffel arrived.

"I didn't see any cat burglars outside," she said.

When Clarabel heard the words *cat burglars*, she ran under the TV.

After examining the family room, Officer Wiffel said, "I'll let you know if we find the music box."

"Thank you," said Mr. and Mrs. Twiddle.

The police officer said good night and left.

Collecting Clues

The next morning, Timothy knocked on Tabitha's door.

"Going to a party?" Tabitha asked.

"Don't you recognize Sherlock Holmes, the great detective?" Timothy asked.

Timothy was wearing a cape and a strange hat.

"Come on," said Timothy. "Let's hunt for the cat burglar."

Clarabel ran under Tabitha's bed.

Tabitha took out her magnifying glass. "There must be some clues outside the family room window."

Timothy and Tabitha ran outside and studied the ground. They made a list of what they found.

Tabitha put the clues into her clue box.

"Look at these tracks," Timothy said excitedly.

"Which ones?" Tabitha asked. Most of the footprints were Clarabel's.

"These," said Timothy, pointing.

"They look like a child's footprints," Tabitha said.

"A child cat burglar?" Timothy scratched his head, puzzled.

"A child likes chocolate bars, bananas, and coconuts," said Tabitha. "Do you know a kid with the initials JJ?"

"I can't think of anyone," said Timothy, still studying the ground.

Suddenly Timothy let out a shout. "Look!" he said. "Here's another print. And another. They lead away from the house."

Timothy and Tabitha followed a line of tracks that circled around the house and circled back and
circled around and
circled back and
circled around.

"I'm getting dizzy," said Tabitha.

CLUES

Finally the tracks led away from the house. Tabitha and Timothy followed them through their neighbors' backyards. Three houses away, Timothy bumped into the Filberts' garbage can. The Filberts were new neighbors.

Timothy's eyes popped. "There's a whole bunch of banana peels in this can."

"And coconut shells!" said Tabitha.

"And chocolate bar wrappers!" said Timothy.

"But the Filberts don't have any children," said Tabitha, puzzled.

As the twins got closer to the house, they saw banana peels outside an open window. Then they heard:

TINKLE. TINKLE. TINKLE.

"Our music box!" they shouted.

Catching the Burglar

Tabitha and Timothy peered through the open window. The music box rested on a table. Standing over the table was an elderly couple.

"Do you think they're cat burglars?" Timothy asked.

Just then several loud, sharp SQUEALS broke out.

"I'm leaving," said Tabitha.

"No you're not," said Timothy. His knees were knocking so hard he couldn't run.

The twins stood trembling together as loud chattering filled the air. A monkey began dancing around the room to the music. Then he suddenly leaped to the window.

"Come back here," shouted Mr. Filbert. "Why, hello," he said, spotting Timothy and Tabitha. "Meet Jo Jo, our new pet."

"JJ!" the twins cried together.

The monkey held out a paw.

"Jo Jo misbehaved last night," said Mr. Filbert. "He jumped out the window, and when he returned he had a music box. He sure does love it."

"If you ever hear about someone missing a music box, please let us know," said Mrs. Filbert. "We want to give it back."

"It's us!" cried Tabitha and Timothy.

"You're the owners?" said Mr. Filbert.

Mrs. Filbert got the music box. "Here, take it," she said.

The twins took the music box reluctantly.

"These belong to Jo Jo," Tabitha said, removing the cap and bow tie from her clue box.

Timothy looked at Tabitha. Then he looked at the Filberts. "We'll be right back," he said. He grabbed Tabitha's hand and they dashed home.

No More Burglars

Tabitha and Timothy ran into the house. "We found the music box!" they shouted to their parents. "The Filberts' pet monkey, Jo Jo, took it."

"Mrs. Filbert gave it back to us, but Jo Jo loves it *so* much," Tabitha said.

"We have an old hand organ in the attic," said Mrs. Twiddle. "The kind that organ grinders used to play. Jo Jo will love it even more."

Mr. Twiddle ran upstairs and came down grinding the organ. "Just tell that monkey," he said, "that in the future our house is off-limits to burglars."

The twins raced back to the Filberts' house and gave Mr. Filbert the hand organ. "Why, thank you!" he exclaimed.

As Mr. Filbert played, Jo Jo whirled happily around the room. He scooped up a banana and a chocolate bar and handed them to the twins.

After watching Jo Jo for a while, the twins started home. All of a sudden, Timothy stopped short. "Oh, no!" he wailed. He pointed to the lawn of their house.

Clarabel had dug up half the lawn searching for her rubber mouse and old flea collar.

“I have
reachi
the
“ME
ran into